This book belongs to:

To everybody who loves wild woods

Also available:

Jack and Boo's Bucket of Treasures

First published in Great Britain by Beachy Books in 2011

Text and photographs copyright © 2011 Philip Bell
Illustrations copyright © 2011 Eleanor Bell

For more information visit
www.beachybooks.com

ISBN: 978-0-9562980-1-0

Jack and Boo's
Wild Wood

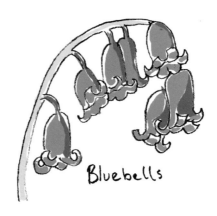

Bluebells

Written by **Philip Bell**   Illustrated by **Eleanor Bell**

Beachy Books

www.beachybooks.com

In ancient woods
under canopy of trees
we forage
like squirrels
from spring to autumn
for new shoots
and summer fruit
windfall seeds
and fallen leaves.

Squirrel

"Fetch girl! Fetch!"

Woof! Woof!

We spot a family walking their dog along a trail overgrown with drifts of wild bluebells.

The dog scampers after a stick thrown into the undergrowth.

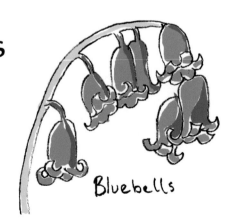

Bluebells

We climb
on a huge fallen
tree trunk, a fungus
filled home to a million
scuttling things
woodlice, earwigs, spiders.

We play to the echo of
distant drumming
woodpeckers carving
nesting hollows.

Garden
Spider

Great
Spotted Woodpecker

We eat sandwiches
on timber thrones carved
by woodland elves.

At the edge of a riverbank
we watch mini dragons fly
pond skaters dance
dabbling ducks
daring ducklings.

Can you count all
the baby ducks?

We collect sticks
to make a secret camp
under an oak tree
blown down in a storm
big branches for arms
knotty roots for toes.

I hide in the den and
leap out to scare Boo!

acorn

Oak

She charges back at me
ready for battle – en garde!

We step out of the cool
gloom into the warmth
of a secret sunlit glade
light for wild flowers
nursery for fledging trees
swaying in the breeze.

Boo wishes she could
fly with the delicate
butterflies
blowing about
like blossom.

We tread carefully to avoid
stinging nettles spilling
over the path to pick
juicy sweet blackberries
Mother Nature's
woodland snacks.

We gobble down the sweet
fruit until our lips turn
purple and our
bellies are
full.

Bramble

Blackberry

The trail winds down to a
wooden bridge across
a boggy stream.

"Who's that trip-trapping
across my bridge?"

"Run Boo!"

We escape before
the snoring woodland
troll wakes up...

Hanging down from the
branch of a tall tree is
a rope swing.

We take turns to
swing under the leaves
higher into the air
rushing back again
sometimes spinning
both of us
giggling.

It's almost dinner time as
we run under the legs of
beech tree giants
home to squirrel dreys
and roosting crows.

Under the shadow of
a lone horse chestnut
tree we collect conkers
shiny reminders
of our adventure
in the Wild Wood.

Horse
Chestnut

conker

Wild Wood Spotter

Oak

acorn

Seven spot ladybird

Sycamore

Great Spotted Woodpecker

Horse Chestnut

nuthatch

Scots pine

cone

conker

Red admiral

Fly agaric

Rabbit

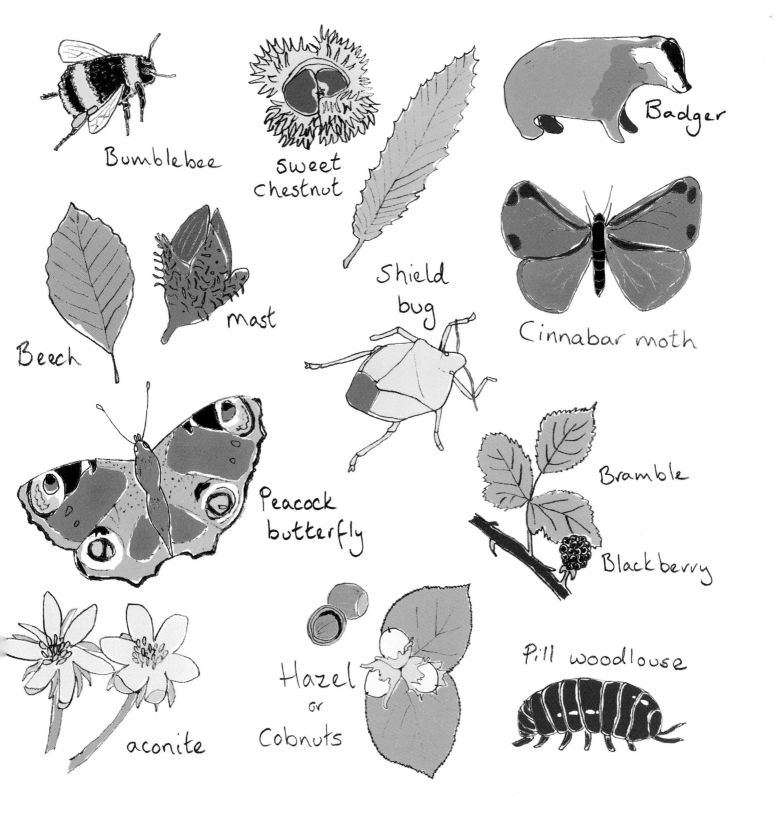

Bumblebee

Sweet chestnut

Badger

Beech

mast

Shield bug

Cinnabar moth

Peacock butterfly

Bramble

Blackberry

aconite

Hazel or Cobnuts

Pill woodlouse

Wild Wood Scavengers

All through the year there are wild things to spot, collect and taste in a local wood near you. Get scavenging then make your own list!

Count the spots on a ladybird.

Take a picture of a butterfly.

Identify an oak tree and collect a leaf or acorn in its cup.

Look under trees in autumn for red and white fly agaric toadstools.

(Don't touch as they are poisonous!)

Taste a blackberry growing on wild brambles.

Can you find Boo the Fairy or Jack the Woodland Elf?

Wild Wood Activities

Make a camp in the wood out of long sticks, or hide out under a fallen tree or hollow. Look out for other animal homes: Insects under rotting logs, or squirrel dreys (nests) high up in the tree, about the size of a football, made of leaves and sticks. Please leave nature as you find it though!

Eat a teddy bear's picnic and listen and watch nature. Sometimes when you keep walking you miss loads and the noise scares the wildlife. Watch for things scurrying through the undergrowth or falling from trees.

Go on a bluebell walk in an ancient woodland during late spring (between March to end of May). Listen for woodpeckers, cuckoos, wood pigeons, owls, bees and nature all around.

Follow the Countryside Code
Be safe, plan ahead and follow any signs.
Leave gates and property as you find them.
Protect plants and animals and take your litter home.
Keep dogs under close control.
Consider other people.

Have Jack and Boo inspired you to explore a Wild Wood near you?

CPSIA information can be obtained
at www.ICGtesting.com
Printed in the USA
LVIC031114310512

2860LVUK00004B